A WONDERFUL WALK

By Josh Yellin and Reid Bogert

ISBN: 978-1-78324-189-7

Final illustrations by Tommy Kho

Published by Wordzworth
www.wordzworth.com

Our story begins
on a day like today,
for a penguin named Pete,
who was well on his way.

Waddle after waddle,
step after step,

Pete walked
with no smile,
his steps
had no pep.

Pete's beak faced down,
and he stared at his toes.

If there was more to see,
he didn't seem to know.

Then suddenly "bump,"
a nut hit Pete's head.

Pete then looked up
and saw his soon-to-be friend.

A walrus named Walter
spoke from up in his tree,

"Greetings, young penguin,
here's a lesson for free!"

"You look down at the ground,"
said Walter the Wise.

"Why not around?
You may be surprised."

"I've walked here before,"
said young penguin Pete.

"There's nothing to see
but rocks and my feet."

"Pete, my boy.
Oh, it's so clear to me.

You've never REALLY looked,
or more you would see!"

Pete was confused,
he had seen things indeed...

some rocks and his feet...
Pete disagreed!

Then Walter exclaimed,
"Look Pete, please LOOK!"

Walter's voice
boomed and the earth
SHOOK, SHOOK.

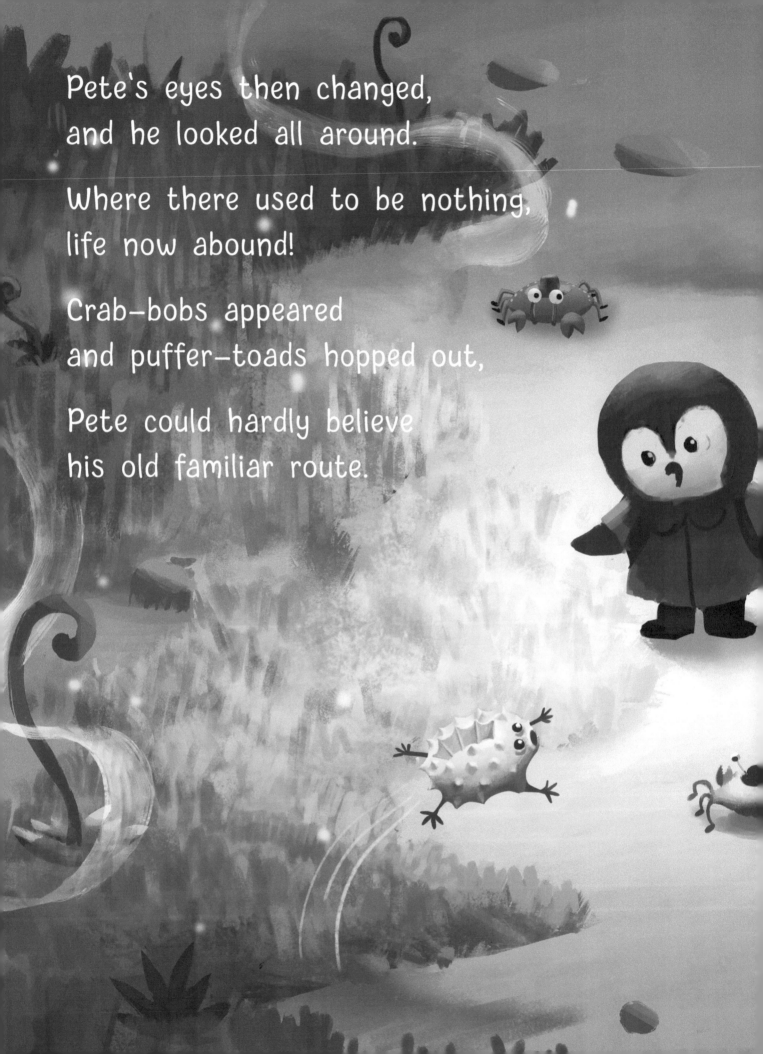

Pete's eyes then changed,
and he looked all around.

Where there used to be nothing,
life now abound!

Crab-bobs appeared
and puffer-toads hopped out,

Pete could hardly believe
his old familiar route.

"Walter, wise walrus,
how could this be?"

"Pete, young penguin,
when you look, you will see!"

The world came
alive with eel-worms
and shark-cats,
seahorse-flies, dog-fins,
fox-rays, and fish-rats.

The world came
alive with eel-worms
and shark-cats,
seahorse-flies, dog-fins,
fox-rays, and fish-rats.

Then the creatures lined up
and they all closed their eyes.

"Walter, what are they doing?
Look here, come on guys!"

"There's much more to the world
than what you can see.

Now close your eyes,
open your ears, and listen closely!"

Pete closed his eyes,
and listen he did.

The crab-bobs still crawled,
the eel-worms still slid.

Then a faint song from the
distance Pete heard,

they all had lined up to hear...
beluga-birds!

The song got louder,
more beautiful and grand.

The song was universal,
one all could understand.

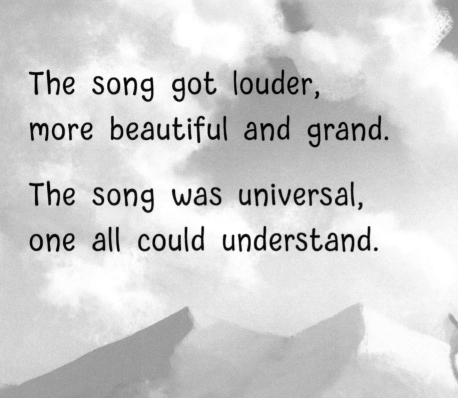

"Open your eyes, my Pete,"
Walter said with a grin.

"Use your eyes,
your ears, and
take it all in!"

Pete looked and listened,
and smiled ear-to-ear.

He could see, he could hear,
it all was so clear!

The beluga–birds flew on,
and their song faded out.

All of the creatures then scattered about.

Then Pete's big smile
fell into a frown.

"Pete, why the sadness?
Why do you feel down?"

"Walter the Wise, I had never before seen or heard the beauty that beluga-birds bring.

Now that they're gone, I'm a little afraid.

When will they come back? I wish they had stayed..."

"Pete, don't worry.
One day they'll return.

But for now look harder,
listen closer, and learn."

"The world around you
will make you say "wow."

for instance, what you lean on
is a big blue whale-cow!"

"And although the big things are easy to see, don't forget the small things are still wondrous indeed.

Look at the krill-grass that the blue whale-cows eat, and you'll see there's a lot more than your eyes first meet."

"The world around you is yours to explore.

Now that you've opened your eyes and ears more.

Continue your walk
and remember, my Pete,

any walk can be wonderful
if you look up from your feet."

Pete waddled along, and although Walter was gone, Pete knew that his wonderful walk would go on.

The End.

CPSIA information can be obtained
at www.ICGtesting.com
Printed in the USA
BVHW061122170821
614611BV00009B/1157